Puffin Books

The dog sniffs Jimmy's legs.
Jimmy sniffs the dog's legs.
The dog sniffs Jimmy's bottom.
Jimmy sniffs ... aaargh.

Horrible, horrible, horrible.

It's a dog's life for Jimmy
when the gizmo gets really gross.

A third gizmo yarn from
Australia's master of madness.

Other books by Paul Jennings

Unreal
Unbelievable
Quirky Tails
Uncanny
The Cabbage Patch Fib and *The Cabbage Patch War*
(both illustrated by Craig Smith)
The Paw Thing
(illustrated by Keith McEwan)
Unbearable
Round the Twist
Unmentionable
Undone
The Gizmo, The Gizmo Again and *Sink the Gizmo*
(all illustrated by Keith McEwan)
The Paul Jennings Superdiary
Uncovered
Wicked (with Morris Gleitzman)
Unseen
Uncollected

Picture Books

Grandad's Gifts
(illustrated by Peter Gouldthorpe)
Round the Twist
(graphic novel with Glenn Lumsden
and David de Vries)
The Fisherman and the Theefyspray
(illustrated by Jane Tanner)
Spooner or Later, Duck for Cover and *Freeze a Crowd*
(all with Ted Greenwood and Terry Denton)

Paul Jennings

*Illustrated
by Keith McEwan*

PUFFIN BOOKS

Puffin Books
Penguin Books Australia Ltd,
487 Maroondah Highway, PO Box 257
Ringwood, Victoria 3134, Australia
Penguin Books Ltd,
Harmondsworth, Middlesex, England
Penguin Putnam Inc.
375 Hudson Street, New York, New York 10014, USA
Penguin Books Canada Limited,
10 Alcorn Avenue, Toronto, Ontario, Canada M4V 3B2
Penguin Books (N.Z.) Ltd,
Cnr Rosedale and Airborne Roads, Albany, Auckland, New Zealand
Penguin Books (South Africa) (Pty) Ltd
5 Watkins St, Denver Ext 4, 2094, South Africa
Penguin Books India (P) Ltd
11, Community Centre, Panchsheel Park,
New Delhi 110 017, India

First published by Penguin Books Australia, 1996
10 9 8 7 6 5 4
Copyright © Greenleaves Pty Ltd, 1996
Illustrations Copyright © Keith McEwan, 1996

Typeset in Palatino by Midland Typesetters, Maryborough, Victoria
Made and printed in Australia by Australian Print Group, Maryborough, Victoria

National Library of Australia
Cataloguing-in-Publication data:

Jennings, Paul, 1943–
Come back gizmo.

ISBN 0 14 037845 6.

1. Dogs - Juvenile fiction. I. McEwan,
Keith II, Title.

A823.3

www.puffin.com.au

To all those who work for the RSPCA

K.M.

.Oh, what will I do? Who will save me? I try to speak but only a growl comes out. And I am busting. I need to have a leak. I stagger over to the wall and start to pee. I scribble out a little message that starts to run down the wall.

There she is again.

Thump, thump, thump, thump. My heart is racing. My face is red. It's the girl next door. Oh, just look at her. Golden hair. Blue eyes. White, white teeth.

Boy, is she beautiful.

She would never even look at a jerk like me. Not a boy with a pimple right on the end of his nose. And not a dollar to his name.

Samantha is carrying her cat, Doddles. It's one of those expensive ones with green eyes. It is a classy cat. There is nothing cheap about it. It is a purebred. It probably cost a fortune. Not like my dog, Biscuit. He is not a purebred. He is a bit of this and a bit of that. He is a good dog, though. He can roll over and play dead. To be perfectly honest I think there is a bit of mongolian wolfhound in him. Dad thinks there could be a touch of dingo, too. Mum says he is mostly rabbit because he digs holes all the time.

There goes the girl of my dreams. Samantha. What a wonderful name. I have a photo of her in my pocket. I took it with my camera when she wasn't looking. Every night I give the photo a little kiss before I go to sleep. On the back I have written *JIMMY 4 SAMANTHA*.

I have never kissed a girl, you know. Never. Thirteen and never been kissed. Don't get me wrong. I don't want to kiss just anyone. It would have to be Samantha or no one.

Samantha, Samantha, Samantha. I close my eyes and pretend that I am kissing her lovely lips. They are soft, soft, soft. She would never give me a kiss. I know that. What about a smile, though? She might give me a smile. I am so much in love with her that I would probably settle for a smile.

'Arf, arf, arf.' My daydream is destroyed. Biscuit is barking. Oh no. He is over at the fence jumping up at Samantha. He is trying to get at Doddles. Biscuit is not really fond of cats.

Oh, this is bad. This is terrible. Samantha will not like this. Not one bit. I have to do something. And quick. 'Here, Biscuit,' I yell. 'Here, boy. Come on, come on. Down, boy. Down.'

Biscuit does not take one scrap of notice. He keeps jumping and barking. Doddles is becoming scared. Her back arches up like a bridge. She starts to spit and hiss. What if she scratches Samantha?

I race inside and grab Biscuit's lead. I fix it to his collar and start to drag him away. But he does not want to come. He puts on the brakes. He digs his feet into the ground. Samantha glares at me. It is not a nice look. 'You are pathetic,' she says. 'Can't you stop that mongrel barking?'

Samantha will never forgive me for this. I will never get a kiss now. I will never even get a smile. Biscuit is disgracing us. He is frightening poor little Doddles.

What will I do?

'Put it in the car,' yells Samantha. She is pointing at Dad's old Ford.

'It's locked,' I gasp. This is embarrassing. What must Samantha think of me?

'Shove it in the boot,' she says.

The boot? In with the spare wheel? It's dark in there. And hot. And there's not much air. Samantha is getting angry. Her beautiful cheeks are turning red. I don't want to be in her bad books. So I open the boot and shove poor old Biscuit inside. I slam down the lid before he can get out.

There is a bit of a muffled bark from inside the car. Then everything grows quiet. Poor old Biscuit. What have I done? I've put my best friend in the boot – that's what. I feel bad. As if I've done something really, really mean. My conscience is nagging at me. I try not to listen to it, and look at the girl of my dreams.

'That's better,' says Samantha. She strokes Doddles and gives her a little kiss. Lucky Doddles.

'I'm sorry, Samantha,' I say. 'Biscuit is a good dog really.'

Samantha looks at me as if I am a worm. She shakes her head as if she cannot believe what I have just said. 'Come with me,' she says.

She turns around and walks towards her house. I just stand there with my mouth hanging open. She stops and glares at me. 'What are you waiting for?' she says.

'Me?' I say.

'I can't see anyone else,' she says. 'Can you?'

Oh, this is good. Samantha is inviting me into her house. Me, Jimmy Rickets. I can't believe my luck. I hurry into her front yard and walk past their Mercedes Benz. Then I follow Samantha into her house.

Samantha lives in a big double-storey house. There is expensive furniture everywhere. The carpet is soft and pink. The walls are lined with pictures in gold frames. I feel very shy. I bet the pimple on my nose is glowing like a lighthouse.

'Right,' says Samantha. 'I want you to do me a favour.'

She is so forceful, is Samantha. She looks especially beautiful with this strong look on her face. I feel weak at the knees. I can't believe that she is actually talking to me. She pulls a piece of paper out of a drawer and writes on it.

I wonder what she wants me to do. I will do anything for her. Anything.

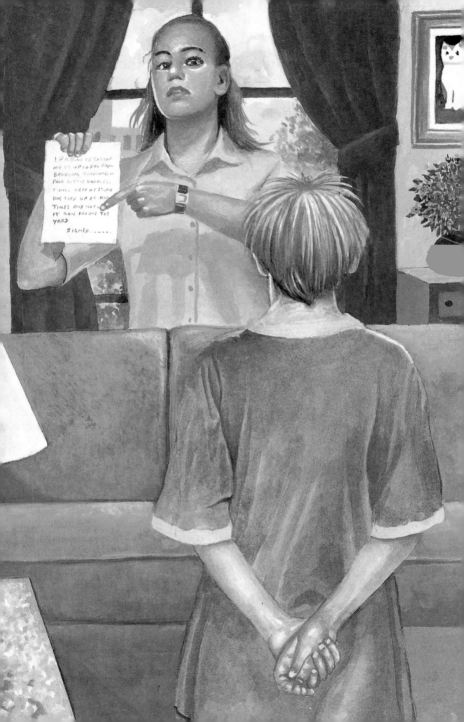

She stops writing and hands me the paper. This is what it says:

I PROMISE TO STOP MY STUPID DOG FROM BARKING AND CHASING POOR LITTLE DODDLES. I WILL KEEP MY STUPID DOG TIED UP AT ALL TIMES AND NOT LET IT RUN AROUND THE YARD.

SIGNED.........

'You have to sign your name there,' she says.

I look into her lovely blue eyes. 'But Biscuit likes running around the yard,' I say.

Samantha sighs. She is so beautiful when she sighs. 'Yes, but Doddles likes to walk in your place for some reason. And your mutt chases her off.'

I think about poor old Biscuit being locked up all the time. Then I look into Samantha's smiling face. It is hard to resist her.

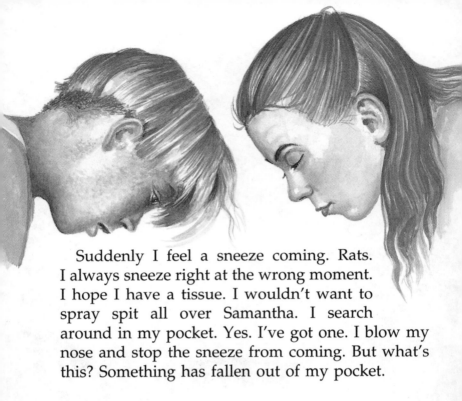

Suddenly I feel a sneeze coming. Rats.
I always sneeze right at the wrong moment.
I hope I have a tissue. I wouldn't want to
spray spit all over Samantha. I search
around in my pocket. Yes. I've got one. I blow my
nose and stop the sneeze from coming. But what's
this? Something has fallen out of my pocket.

We both stare at it.

Oh, no. No, no, no. It isn't. It is. I am so
embarrassed. I can't move. Samantha bends down
and picks up the photo. She looks at her picture and
then turns it over. She reads where it says *JIMMY
4 SAMANTHA*.

'Ah ha,' she says. She stares at me with a grin. 'Close your eyes, JIMMY.'

She used my name. Oh, she looks so beautiful when she uses my name. I close my eyes. What is she going to do? Is this a game? Is she giving me a present? Suddenly I feel something soft and wonderful touching my lips. Oh, I am in heaven. She is kissing me. She is really kissing me. The kiss only lasts for a second. But it fills me up like Coke inside a bottle. I am full of fizz and sweetness.

I open my eyes. 'Now,' she says. 'Now will you sign the agreement?'

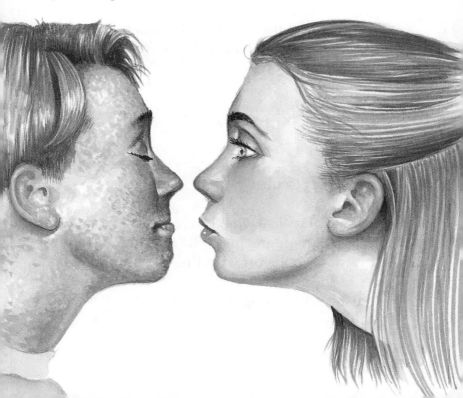

Will I sign the agreement? I will do anything for her. My head is spinning. I touch my lips where hers have touched mine. I don't care about anything. I pick up the pencil and sign on the dotted line.

She inspects the signature with a sniff. 'You can go now,' she says. She leads me to the front door and before I know it she has shown me out. 'Remember,' she says. 'You have signed an agreement. You have to keep that dog locked up.' She shuts the door with a bang.

I walk down the path in a dream. She kissed me. My first kiss. I have kissed a girl. Whoo-ee. Ya-hoo.

Somehow or other I force my shaking legs to take me into our place. I had better let poor old Biscuit out of the car boot.

The car.

It is gone.

And so is Biscuit.

Suddenly I realise what I have done. I have signed a piece of paper agreeing to tie my dog up for ever. And Dad has gone off with Biscuit shut in the boot.

I have sold my dog down the river for a kiss.

2

I race into the house. 'Mum,' I shout. 'Mum, where's Dad gone?'

There is no answer. Mum is not home. And neither is Dad. They have gone out somewhere. With Biscuit in the boot. What if he suffocates? There isn't much air in a boot. It is a hot day and he won't have anything to drink. They might be gone for ages. Biscuit might die. If only I could go back to before I shut him in the boot.

Where could they have gone? Think. Think. They could have gone around to Dad's mate Ralph's house. They won't come back from there for hours. Dad will be mucking around with fishing rods all day.

Calm. Stay calm. Think, think. I sit down and make a list of all the places they could have gone. The movies. The beach. The golf club. Ralph's. Jennie's. Auntie Hillary's. I rush over to the phone and ring everywhere they might be. But no one has seen Dad or the car.

I will just have to sit and wait.

It is ten o'clock in the morning. They might not come back until tea-time. Poor old Biscuit might be in the boot for eight hours. He could die in that time. What have I done?

An hour goes by. And then another. I turn on the television but I don't really watch it. I just think about my dog.

Suddenly I hear a car door slam. They are back. I rush over to the window but my heart falls. It is not Dad's Ford. It is a small van. It has RSPCA written on the side. I know what that stands for – *Royal Society for the Prevention of Cruelty to Animals.*

I race outside and see a little man wearing glasses. His eyes flash as if there is lightning inside his head. To be honest he gives me the creeps. He walks around to the back of the van and opens the door.

Biscuit jumps out. Oh, this is wonderful. My prayers are answered. 'Biscuit, Biscuit, Biscuit,' I yell. I am so happy. He runs up and starts licking my hands and jumping all over me. I am so glad to see him. He is okay. Everything is all right.

'Who owns this dog?' says the man with the weird eyes.

'He does,' says a voice. It is the beautiful Samantha. She has come over to see what is going on.

The little man looks at me through his glasses. There is thunder and lightning inside his head. 'We found this dog whimpering in the boot of a car at the railway station,' he says. 'The poor thing was half dead. Whose idea was it to put the dog in the boot?'

'His,' says the beautiful Samantha. She points straight at me.

'It was a cruel thing to do,' says the little man. 'I will have to speak to your father.'

'He's out,' says Samantha. 'So buzz off, Pop.'

Samantha looks beautiful when she is angry. But she is only making things worse.

I open my mouth to explain everything but the little man holds up his hand. 'Very well,' he says. 'But I will be back.' He steps into his van and starts the engine. Then he does something weird. 'Here, boy,' he says. He throws a ball out into the garden. Biscuit goes racing after it. Biscuit loves chasing balls. And he will never give them back.

Samantha starts to walk off. 'Remember your promise,' she says to me.

I touch my lips and remember that kiss. What I wouldn't do for another.

I turn around to say goodbye to the little man. But I am too late. He has gone. And I didn't even see him go.

I take Biscuit inside into my bedroom. He has the ball in his mouth. 'Give it to me, Biscuit,' I say. Biscuit backs off. He never gives up a ball. It is the weirdest looking ball I have ever seen. It seems to have little windows in it. There are little crackles inside its windows. They are like flashes of lightning. It is not a ball at all. It is some sort of electrical gizmo. Little green and red lights are flashing on the sides.

I reach down to grab the gizmo but Biscuit won't let go. He growls and starts to pull away. Suddenly the gizmo beeps.

3

Everything changes. Everything. The beep from the gizmo has changed my world. What is it? What has happened? I blink and rub my eyes. The room is the same. But different.

'No, no,' I yell. I sit down on my bed. Everything is black and white and grey. There is no colour in the room. My blue T-shirt is grey. My yellow shorts are grey. Biscuit is grey.

I am colour-blind. Why? What caused it?

The kiss? Surely not. You can't go colour-blind from kissing a girl. Can you? I rush over to the mirror and look at my eyes. They are different. I can't tell what colour they are. But they are different. A funny shape. They look bigger.

Biscuit is running around the kitchen with the gizmo still in his mouth. He is going crazy. His tail is wagging like mad. I have never known him to be like this. He is sniffing everything in the place as if he had never seen it before. He seems very happy.

I need help. I am sick. All I did was kiss a girl and now I am colour-blind. What if it is some terrible disease? I must tell Mum and Dad before something else happens. But they aren't here. I must find them. Where could they be? My mind is spinning. I can't think straight. Where are they? Where, where, where? Their car is at the station. They always leave it there when they go to the pub for a counter lunch. Dad won't drive the car after a few beers.

They will be at Rafferty's. I head for the station as quickly as I can go. And Biscuit runs after me. Oh no. I promised Samantha that I would tie him up. 'Go home, boy,' I say.

Biscuit does not go home. He just grips the gizmo in his mouth and runs after me. 'Quick,' I say. 'Before Samantha sees you.' But it is too late. She is looking out of the window. She has seen us.

Right at that very minute the gizmo beeps. I feel funny. Biscuit stands rock still like a statue. I feel like there is electricity in my brain. Something weird is going on. But what?

Suddenly I feel the urge to scratch. I am itchy. Right between the legs. Not just a little bit itchy. Enormously itchy. I have to scratch it. But Samantha is looking. Don't scratch. Don't, don't. But I do. I shove my hand inside my shorts and have a scratch. I just can't stop myself.

And Samantha is looking. She closes the curtains in disgust. She thinks I am revolting. Oh, now I have done it. I will never get another kiss. Not as long as I live. A boy who scratches himself down there in public is the pits. There is something wrong with me. I need help. I must find my parents. Quickly.

I run for the station as fast as I can go. There is no time to take Biscuit home. He will just have to come with me. I stop to scratch. Biscuit does not scratch. He looks as if he has never had a flea in his life.

We reach the station and I sit down panting on a bench. 'Good boy,' I say. 'It's not your fault. You are a good dog.' Biscuit stares into my eyes. I stare into his.

What? His eyes are different too. They seem smaller. A cold feeling crawls across my skin. The world is going crazy. The gizmo beeps again. I feel electricity in my brain again.

I have to get rid of that gizmo. It seems to beep about every ten minutes. And every time it does things get worse. 'Biscuit,' I shout. 'Give me that thing.' But Biscuit just backs off along the platform. I can't get at it. He is too quick for me.

Nearby is a flowerbed. Someone has gone to a lot of trouble to plant it out with hundreds of grey flowers. Suddenly I feel an urge. I am pulled towards the flowerbed. I don't want to go but I just can't stop myself. I start digging in the flowerbed with my hands. I go crazy sending dirt and flowers everywhere.

Dig, dig, dig, dig. Why am I doing this? Dirt flies over other people nearby.

'Vandal,' says a little old lady.

Just then the train pulls in and passengers step

off. I should jump onto the train but I can't stop digging until I have found what I am after. But what am I after? Dirt is flying everywhere. More and more people are showered with it. My fingers are sore with the effort.

'Hey,' says a loud voice. It is the guy in charge of the station. Boy, is he mad. 'Cut that out,' he yells. He waves a fist at me. 'What are you doing, you little brat?'

I scratch around in the dirt. 'Looking for this,' I say.

I hold up a dirty old bone. Then I put it in my mouth and stare at them all.

Everyone on the station is looking at me with horrified faces. They can't believe what they are seeing. The station guy is boiling with rage. He runs over to a wall and grabs a bucket with FIRE written on the side. 'Cop this,' he yells. He throws the bucket of water all over me.

The train is leaving. The doors are shutting. Quick as a flash I jump on board. Biscuit follows me. 'Hey,' yells the station guy. 'No dogs are allowed on the ..' His voice trails off as the train gathers speed.

Biscuit curls up on the seat. No one takes any notice of him. They are all staring at me. I am covered in dirt. And soaking wet.

There is no towel for me to use. I don't want to

use one anyway. I don't need it. I just stand there and shake myself like someone twirling a wet mop. No, more like someone drying out an umbrella. No, that's not right either. I shake myself like Biscuit does when he has been for a swim in the sea.

The passengers all moan and groan as water sprays all over them.

A tough-looking guy shakes a fist at me. 'You dirty dog,' he says.

4

Oh, this is weird. This is scary. What is going on here? I am starting to act like a dog. I scratched myself in public. I dug up a bone. I shook myself dry. Oh, I don't like this one little bit. But Biscuit does. He is getting happier by the minute.

I jump off the train and head for Rafferty's. Oh, I do hope Mum and Dad are there. Biscuit follows with the gizmo still in his mouth. We walk through grey streets. We pass grey houses and grey people. Why can't I see colours any more? What is wrong with my eyes? Stay calm. Think, Jimmy, think.

A terrible thought starts to crawl into my mind. Oh no. It can't be. No, no, no. Dogs don't see in colour. Dogs are colour-blind. I am starting to act like a dog. The gizmo is doing it. Making me feel what it is like to be a dog.

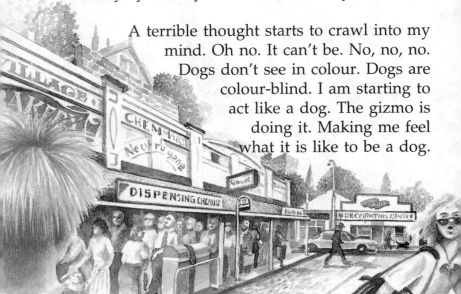

We have to get rid of the gizmo. I shudder to think what might happen if we don't.

'Here, Biscuit. Good dog,' I say. Biscuit comes over for a pat. I stroke his head. Then, quick as lightning I snatch at the ball. My fingers close around it but Biscuit hangs on tight. I try to pull the gizmo from Biscuit's mouth. It is all covered in horrible dog saliva.

'Let go,' I yell. 'Let go.' But Biscuit does not let go. He knows when he is onto a good thing. He growls and pulls backwards. It is almost as if he likes this gizmo thing. We roll over on the ground, fighting over the gizmo. Suddenly it beeps. A little electric shock goes through my brain. 'Aargh,' I yell. I release the gizmo and climb to my feet.

'Okay,' I say to Biscuit. 'Keep it then, but you'll be sorry.'

I don't know how wrong I am. Biscuit is not going to be sorry. But I am.

We walk on down the street. As we go past a lamp-post I suddenly lift up one leg. 'What did I do that for?' We go past another lamp-post and I lift up my leg again. Every time we go past a lamp-post I cock up a leg. Oh, shame. Shame, shame, shame. There are lamp-posts everywhere. Passers-by look at me as if I am crazy. I just can't stop myself cocking up a leg at the lamp-post.

I have to hurry. I pant as I run along the street. My tongue hangs out and flaps in the breeze. It makes my cheeks all wet.

This is weird but I don't have any time to think about it. Another dog is coming along the street. A scruffy, hairy old thing that looks like it has just been digging in a rubbish bin. It is on a lead held by a huge man in army boots. Biscuit is not the least bit interested. But I am. Suddenly I drop down onto all fours. I start to sniff at this dog. The man in the army boots tries to pull his dog away from me. 'Here, Scraggle,' he says. 'Come back, boy.'

But it does not go back. It is very interested in me. It starts to sniff back. Sniff, sniff, sniff, sniff. It sniffs my nose. I sniff its nose. It sniffs my legs. I sniff its legs. It sniffs my tummy. I sniff its tummy. It sniffs my bottom. I sniff ... 'Aaaaaarghhhhhhhhh.'

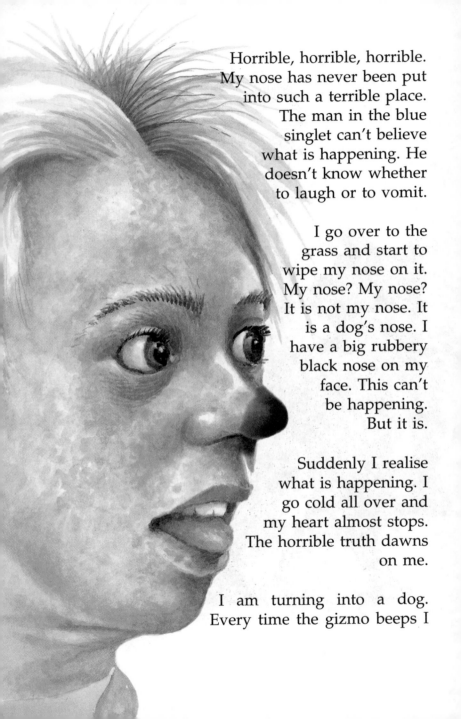

Horrible, horrible, horrible. My nose has never been put into such a terrible place. The man in the blue singlet can't believe what is happening. He doesn't know whether to laugh or to vomit.

I go over to the grass and start to wipe my nose on it. My nose? My nose? It is not my nose. It is a dog's nose. I have a big rubbery black nose on my face. This can't be happening. But it is.

Suddenly I realise what is happening. I go cold all over and my heart almost stops. The horrible truth dawns on me.

I am turning into a dog. Every time the gizmo beeps I

grow more dog-like. It is turning me into a dog. I have to get away from that gizmo. Even if it means leaving Biscuit behind.

Biscuit. Look at him. He has a pink nose. And pink ears.

'Aargh,' I scream. 'Aargh, aargh, aargh.' I am turning into Biscuit. And he is turning into me. We are swapping bits. Every time the gizmo beeps he gets more like me and I grow more like him.

Biscuit trots happily over to a rock.

I wish.

Biscuit *walks* over to a rock. On two legs. Like a human being. He walks over and sits down. Then he crosses his legs and looks at me. Through my eyes.

'Aaaaargh,' I scream. 'Please help.'

Biscuit does not look too upset. Why should he? His world is coloured. He is probably glad that he is turning into a person.

I am turning into a dog. I am terrified. And I am lonely. My future flashes in front of me. I will never sleep in a bed. I will never kiss a girl. I will never watch TV. Or go into a hamburger shop. My life will be full of lamp-posts, cold nights and rubbish-bin meals. Horrible, horrible, horrible. Mum, Mum, Mum. Oh, I want my mum. I must get to the pub as quickly as I can. Before it

is too late. Before no
one can recognise
me at all.

5

I tear down the street. My feet fly. I have never run so fast in my life. I am in a panic. My tongue flops out sending a spray of spit out behind me. At every lamp-post I screech to a halt and cock up a leg. Why am I doing that? I have no time to stop. But I can't help myself. Biscuit is pounding behind me on two legs. He has my face. Yes – my face. His little mouth can hardly hold the gizmo. Why doesn't he drop the stupid thing?

Because he doesn't want to – that's why. People have better lives than dogs. Plenty of food. Warm beds. No fleas. Free to come and go. No one tying you up. Or putting you in the boot. He is happy to be human.

'Please, Biscuit,' I say. 'I don't like this.'

'Ruff, ruff,' he barks. Or was that 'rough, rough'? No, it couldn't have been. Biscuit has a human mouth. But he doesn't know any words. He can't talk. And he can't give a proper bark either.

'Drop it,' I don't say. I try to say it but only a sort of strangled growl comes out. A dog's mouth is made for barking. Not for talking. Neither of us can talk.

Please let me wake up. Please let it be a dream. Please don't let it be real. Mum, Dad. Be in the pub. You have to be in the pub. Wait for me. Wait for me. I'm coming.

People stare at us as we run by. A little girl screams in horror and drops her ice-cream. She thinks I am a monster. I am a monster. The gizmo is still beeping away in Biscuit's mouth. It has speeded up. It beeps about every two minutes. And every time it does something else changes. I am so unhappy. This is the end of my life. As a boy, that is.

Biscuit smiles with his little pink mouth. But he doesn't wag his tail. He doesn't have a tail.

But I do. It curls out of my shorts and waves in the breeze. A long hairy tail. I am a boy-dog. Half boy and half dog. And Biscuit is a dog-boy. We are two horrible monsters running down the street.

People scream and run away as they see us. 'Get the police,' someone yells.

'Call the army,' shouts a man as he slams his car

door and speeds off in fright.

Oh, how far is it to the pub? Not far. Not far at all. Just around the corner. I run. I cock up a leg. I run a bit more. I cock up another leg.

Oh, Mum. Oh, Dad. Where are you? They will fix everything up. That is what parents are for. They help you when you are sick. They stick up for you when everyone else is against you. Once I find Mum and Dad everything will be okay. And I am nearly there.

Biscuit jogs after me. Except it is not Biscuit any more. He has my legs. My face. My hands. And I have his. I drop down onto all fours, and my shoes drop off. I am all dog. I smell of dog. I have a dog nose. And dog ears. I even have a dog's bottom. This is a nightmare. This is the most horrible thing in the history of the world. Oh, please let me wake up.

I open my mouth to scream out 'Mum, Mum, Mum'. But all that comes out is 'woof, woof, woof'.

People stare at us. They point but they don't seem frightened any more. All they see is a boy and a dog. They don't know that the dog is me. Some of them are laughing. There is a little girl out with her mother. The woman looks disgusted and claps a hand over her daughter's eyes. I look at Biscuit to see what is wrong. No, I look at Biscuit in my body. He is naked. That used to be my body and now it is running naked down the street.

I am finding it difficult to trot. My shorts and T-shirt are too big for a dog. My underpants are twisting around my legs. Biscuit's body just doesn't fit into my clothes.

Oh, will this never end? Yes, yes, yes. There it is. Rafferty's pub. I burst inside and Biscuit follows. There's Mum sitting at a table having a beer with Dad. At last everything will be okay. In any second I will be safe in Mum's arms.

Mum and Dad look up as we burst in. 'Jimmy,' shouts Mum. 'What are you thinking of, boy?'

I open my jaw to answer but then I see something strange. At first I can't take it in. Mum is not looking at me. She is looking at Biscuit. She thinks Biscuit is me. Of course. He is inside my body. And I am inside his.

All the people in the pub are staring. A waitress drops a tray of drinks. A group of young women start to laugh. An elderly man cries out in horror.

Dad is staring at Biscuit. 'Where are your clothes, son?' he yells. 'Why are you in the nude?'

'Over here,' I want to say. 'Look over here. This is me. Your son. Your own boy. Your own flesh and blood.' But 'woof, woof, woof' is all that comes out of my mouth.

Finally Mum does look at me. 'The dog's wearing his clothes,' she shrieks. 'He's put his clothes on Biscuit.' She whips the tablecloth off the table and tries to wrap it around Biscuit who is standing there nude in my body. Biscuit does not want to be wrapped up. He gives a sort of growl-bark and heads for the door. He doesn't mind being in the nude. Dogs are always in the nude – even when they are not dogs.

'Get that pooch out of here,' yells a man behind the bar. He does not mean Biscuit. He means me. Dad comes towards me. 'Get out of here, Biscuit,' he yells.

My own father. Chasing me outside. Can't you see it's me? Jimmy. Your boy. No, he can't see it is me. Dad never lets Biscuit come inside the house. It makes him mad when I smuggle Biscuit into my bedroom. And now he thinks that Biscuit is in the pub.

The man behind the bar comes towards me waving a broom. 'Get off, you mutt,' he shouts.

This is dangerous. I will have to get out of here. I lower my eyes and slink out the door. My tail hangs down between my legs.

Biscuit-boy is already heading down the street. Still in the nude. Mum and Dad chase after him. They think he is me. 'Come back, Jimmy,' calls Mum. 'Come and put your clothes on. It's all right. We are not going to hurt you.'

The drinkers from the pub all rush outside to watch the chase. No one is interested in me. I am on my own. I could go rushing after them. But what's the point? They will only chase me off. Or lock me up. I have to figure out what to do.

Poor old Biscuit is scared at all the fuss. He runs

off with my body. Mum and Dad run after him. As they all disappear into the distance I notice one thing. Biscuit-boy is not carrying the gizmo any more. It is gone.

'Git outta here, you mongrel,' yells the man with the broom. I scamper away as fast as I can go.

Mongrel. Mutt. That's what they think of me. No one knows that I am a boy. I feel so lonely. There is no one to talk to. No one to help. I can't even make friends with other dogs. Inside my doggy body I am a boy. A boy crying a million tears.

6

What am I going to do? I can't talk. I can't even write because my paws won't hold a pen. I could scratch a message out in the dust. But would anyone believe me? 'Help,' I could write. 'I am really a boy, not a dog.' Someone might believe it. Or they might think I am the smartest dog in the world. They could put me in a circus or something.

My mind is spinning. I can't think. I put my head back and let out a terrible, sad howl. Like a dingo calling to the moon.

Oh, I can't stand it. I want my mum and dad. I want to be human again. Sad dog tears run down my jaw and plop onto my paws. I crawl under a bush and put my head on my front legs. I don't know what to do.

Think, think, think. No one else is going to help me. I am on my own. I will just have to trot home. In the end I might be able to get a message to Dad or Mum. But then what? Dad doesn't know how to turn a dog back into a boy. No, I must work this out myself.

I scratch my stomach with my back leg. The fleas are driving me crazy. Still, I can't worry about them. I go into deep thought.

The gizmo. The answer is with the gizmo. Yes. That's it. Of course. It just might work. I have to get the gizmo back. But where is it? Biscuit dropped it somewhere along the way. I have to find the gizmo.

I trot along the path retracing my paw steps. I can smell everything. Every lamp-post has the scent of a dog. Every now and then I stop and sniff. I can smell all sorts of things. My sense of smell is fantastic. Dad and Mum are about a mile away. I can pick up their scent on the breeze.

I move along past the pub. Back the way I came. I must find that gizmo. If I get it back it might just save me. I sniff the air. The gizmo. It is not too far off. I put my nose to the ground and follow the trail back the way we came.

Nothing can stop me now.

Suddenly a cat steps out from a driveway. Everything goes crazy inside my head. I start to race after the cat. 'Woof, woof, woof.' I bark like a wild animal. I just can't help myself. The cat scrambles up a tree and I try to follow. I leap like a crazy dog trying to get at the cat.

What am I talking about? *Like* a crazy dog? I *am* a crazy dog. Everything inside me wants to get that cat. I just can't help it. The cat spits and hisses down at me.

I must go. I must find the gizmo. I will never get out of this dog's body if I don't. I will spend the rest of my life in a hairy hell. The cat is like a magnet pulling me back but I manage to drag myself away and trot down the road. I sniff and sniff. Yes, it is far off but I can still smell the gizmo. Way in the distance. Where are you? Come back, gizmo. I need you.

I trot on and on.

The smell of the gizmo becomes stronger and stronger. There are smells, interesting smells. They call me from every lamp-post but I manage to resist them. After a bit the gizmo smell grows weaker. I have gone past it. Yes, back there. I follow my nose along the footpath.

There is something in the long grass. Yes, yes, yes. There it is. The gizmo. But it is not beeping. Oh no. I need it to beep. It is my only hope.

I pick up the gizmo in my mouth and hide in the long grass. I just lie there and wait.

My stomach growls. I am hungry. I wonder what is for tea. Spaghetti and meat sauce. A hamburger and eggs. Not for me. No way. It will be horrible brown stuff out of a tin. Scraped into a bowl in the backyard. Raw and cold. Yuck.

I start to think about other things. How did all of this happen? The gizmo has let me know what it feels like to be a dog. Because I put Biscuit in the car boot. It was a mean thing to do. How I wish that I could go back to before I did it. Poor old Biscuit. And now he is running around in my body. In the nude. He won't know why everyone is chasing him. He will be upset. I bet he wishes he was a dog again by now. It's hard being a kid, too. That's what Biscuit is finding out right now.

I prick up my ears. I sniff the air. Biscuit-boy is coming, I can smell him. He has shaken off Mum and Dad. There he is, running for his life. A naked boy with a dog inside. A great crowd of people are yelling and screaming. There are police cars and even a fire-engine. They are nearly up to him. Poor old Biscuit. He is terrified. All that noise and fuss. Quick as a flash I dash out in front of him. Biscuit-boy knows it is me. In some doggy sort of way he

recognises himself. Yes, he is following me. I dash
back and grab the gizmo in my jaws. Then I bolt
into a drainpipe. The naked Biscuit-boy follows me.
I give a little bark and Biscuit-boy seems to know
that it means 'faster, faster'.

Down into the dark, dark tunnel we go. There is
shouting and yelling behind us. We have to hurry.
Soon the mob will get torches and follow. We need

a moment alone. With the gizmo.

I can see quite well in the dark. But Biscuit-boy can't. Not with my human eyes. He grabs onto my tail and we go on and on. Finally I stop. We fall to the floor of the drain, panting and puffing.

Oh, what will I do? Who will save me? I try to speak but only a growl comes out. And I am busting. I need to have a leak. I stagger over to the wall and start to pee. I scribble out a little message that starts to run down the wall.

HELP.

The gizmo is still tight in my jaws. It is flashing blue and green. Soon it will beep.

I hope.

This is what I have figured out. The man with the lightning eyes set the gizmo to beep at various times. Every time that it goes off Biscuit and I swap parts. Well, what is left? I have all of Biscuit. Head, tail, paws, ears – the lot. Except for one thing.

His brain.

I do not have his brain and he does not have mine. So what is there left to swap? Only our brains. Only our brains. That is all there is left to swap. If Biscuit's brain comes back into this body he will be all back together. And so will I. But we need one more beep to do it. And the gizmo has gone quiet. Please, gizmo, please. Give one last one beep.

There is a lot of noise coming from the end of the drain. They are coming. Soon they will grab Biscuit and take him away. They will not know that it is a dog in a boy's body. They will just think it is me, gone crazy.

If only the gizmo would give one more beep. If only it will swap our brains. Come on, come on, come on.

'Beep.'

Yes, yes, yes. It gave a beep. But it is so dark that I can't see a thing. What has happened? Am I a boy or am I a dog? Did it work?

The crowd are coming. They are holding torches. A man leans down and looks at us. I cower down. Then I see who it is.

Dad.

I can tell it is him by his yellow hat.

7

Oh, it is good to be a boy again. Dad takes me and Biscuit home. Nobody believes that I was a dog. They think it was me running around in the nude. But funnily enough Mum and Dad don't go off crook at me. They are so pleased that I am not acting strangely any more. They actually increase my pocket money.

Life is really strange. Anyway, I am just so glad to be human. Everything goes back to normal. Well, almost everything. Sometimes when I pass a lamp-post I cock up a leg. But only now and then so it doesn't really matter.

Also there is a big fuss in the newspapers. Some people say that they saw a dingo-boy. Others think it was a bunyip. But no one really believes them.

And the gizmo? I put it on the shed roof at the bottom of the yard out of harm's way. Biscuit won't go near it. And I don't blame him.

Not that it stays there for long. Samantha's cat comes over into our yard and runs off with it. Biscuit barks like crazy and chases her off. He is not too worried, though. He is just glad to be his old doggy self. Especially now that Dad lets him come inside at night.

The next morning two things of interest happen.

One, the man with the lightning eyes drives past with a bit of a smile on his face. I give him a wave and he waves back.

Two, Samantha looks over the fence. 'I thought you agreed to tie that mutt up,' she says. She looks at me with those beautiful green eyes. But I don't fall for it.

'Well, I'm not going to,' I say. 'Dogs have feelings too, you know.'

'You promised,' she says.

I shake my head. 'No way. I'm not tying Biscuit up. How would you like being chained up all day? I'm not going to do it.'

Samantha looks at me slyly. 'Not even for a kiss?'

'Not even for a kiss,' I say.

Samantha sticks her nose up in the air and walks off across the lawn.

Boy, she looks beautiful.

Especially when she waves her tail around like that.